For my beautiful children who keep the memory of their father alive.
—P. M. T.

For my mom who always encouraged me to go after my dreams.
—T. J. S.

Special thanks to Tameka Fryer Brown for her helpful suggestions
that brought this story full circle.

To Vanessa Brantley Newton for her artistic suggestions
that both inspired and enlightened.

www.mascotbooks.com

Mother of Many

Text copyright © 2019 by Pamela M. Tuck
Illustrations copyright © 2019 by Tiffani J. Smith

For more information, please contact:
Mascot Books
620 Herndon Parkway #320
Herndon, VA 20170
info@mascotbooks.com

Library of Congress Control Number: 2018915003

CPSIA Code: PRT0219A
ISBN-13: 978-1-64307-439-9

Printed in the United States

MOTHER OF MANY

Written by
Pamela M. Tuck

Illustrated by
Tiffani J. Smith

I heard of a woman who lived in a shoe,
With dozens of children all crammed in there, too.

She fed them some broth,
without any bread.
And when she got mad,
she sent them to bed.

I think this old woman could use some advice,
On how to plan meals and treat children nice.
With thirteen of us, Mom knows what to do.
See, we live in a house, and not some old shoe.

In the morning we rise to the smell of baked bread.
Down in the kitchen, Mom has a nice spread.
Pancakes and bacon, home fries, eggs, and juice,
And oatmeal that Mom always makes a bit loose . . .

. . . for our baby sister,
who's not yet quite two,
The oatmeal's just right for her to chew.

After we've eaten,
we get our chores done.
Mom says that teamwork
is how a home runs.

Mom kisses Daddy,
he heads out the door,
To work for eight hours.
That's Daddy's chore.

After he's gone,
Mom pulls out her list. . .
That even has things
from last week
that we missed!

We grumble. Mom stares
with a hand on her hip.
We know to get busy and
give her no lip.

Jocey heads up to tackle her room.
John grabs a hold of the dustpan and broom.
His job is to sweep, after we eat.
But once Mom is gone, John takes a seat.

Joel empties the trash,
but doesn't come back.

Janae washes dishes so
Jada can stack.

Soon there's a CRASH and a worried, "Oh, my!"
Dishes fall down from stacking too high.

When Mom rushes down, John springs from his chair,
Sweeping so fast, crumbs fly everywhere!
Mom's in the doorway, a frown's on her face.
She says with frustration, "Look at this place."

Then Jeremy yells, "The wash overflowed!
Jared's the one who started that load."
I grab a bucket. Mom grabs a mop.
She opens the lid, so the washer will stop.

Then all of a sudden, Janelle rushes in.
"Rita's playing in the toilet again!"

Mom runs upstairs and finds a big mess.
Wet toilet paper on Rita's new dress.

She cleans up and puts Rita down for a nap.
Mom's barely done when we hear a loud SNAP!

In the boys' room, Mom holds her head.
We both stand and stare at a broken bunk bed.

Mom's looking puzzled.
Jared explains,
"Jordan just wanted
to fly like a plane.

He jumped on the bed,
preparing to soar.
But then the slat broke
and the bed hit the floor."

"That's it!" Mom yells and calls everyone down.
That's when she sees that Joel's not around.
She looks straight at me. "Judah, where did Joel go?"
I shrug my shoulders, 'cause I just don't know.

Just at that moment, Joel rushes in.
Mom glares and says, "Where have you been?"
"I took out the trash, then my friend stopped by.
He brought his new skateboard for me to try."

Mom's voice is gruff, "There's work to be done.
And get to it now. Be finished by one."

The telephone rings. Mom takes the call.
Her voice becomes low as she walks down the hall.

Mom goes to her room. Her door is shut tight.
We all talk about making things right.

Jocey folds laundry and puts it away.
The bathrooms are cleaned by John and Janae.

Janelle picks up toys. Jared vacuums the floor.
Joel grabs a yardstick and heads out the door.

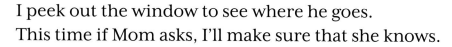

I peek out the window to see where he goes.
This time if Mom asks, I'll make sure that she knows.

He brings a wood plank
out of the shed,
And heads upstairs
to fix the bunk bed.

Jeremy wipes windows.

Jordan lines shoes.

Jada gets furniture
polish to use.
I wipe away dust.
She adds the shine.
Rita wakes up
and starts to whine.

Mom hears Rita
and opens her door.
Her eyes have a sparkle.
She's not mad anymore.

"Daddy just called. He's taking us out."
That's what the whispers were all about.
Mom looks around. A smile's on her face.
She says with delight, "Look at this place."

She checks off her list. We're all feeling pride.
Mom sips her tea as we all head outside.

Soon Daddy's home.
He hears the reports.
(Of course, we don't tell how
things got out of sorts.)

"So, you had a great day."
That's what Daddy thinks.
"It wasn't so bad,"
Mom says with a wink.

We head out to dinner,
all thirteen of us,
Packed in the van
we call the Tuck Bus.

My advice to that woman who lives in the shoe:
Give all your children a chore list to do.
Then you'll have time to make them some bread.
And you'll all be happy when it's time for bed.

About the **Author**

Pamela M. Tuck has been writing poems and stories since she was a child growing up in Greenville, North Carolina. She is the author of *As Fast As Words Could Fly*, the 2007 Lee & Low Books New Voices Award winner. Pamela credits her writing to her upbringing surrounded by southern storytellers. Her family inspires many of her stories. Although Pamela grew up as an only child, she enjoys the excitement of having a large family. Pamela lives in Boyertown, Pennsylvania. Visit her online at pamelamtuck.com.

About the **Illustrator**

Tiffani J. Smith began her passion for art in the early 1990s. She has continued to challenge herself as an artist. Inspired by artists such as Jacob Lawrence, Georges Seurat, Edgar Degas, and Norman Rockwell, Tiffani strives to introduce new techniques while staying true to her traditional artistic roots. She studied traditional graphic design and illustration at Morgan State University, earning a bachelor's degree in fine arts. She has worked as a freelance graphic designer since 1999, creating logos and graphic design for apparel.

Using the traditional mediums as well as digital tools, Tiffani has developed a love for children's illustrations. She enjoys taking a project from a simple thumbnail sketch or idea to a fully integrated, fully developed product. She loves to create whimsical characters and landscapes that speak to every child while still including culturally diverse images. Tiffani has been a dedicated educator who has incorporated the arts in her classroom for the past 14 years.

Originally from Long Island, New York, Tiffani currently resides in Philadelphia, Pennsylvania.